The stockings were hung
By the chimney with care,
In hopes that Saint Nicholas
Soon would be there.

The children were nestled
All snug in their beds,
While visions of sugarplums
Danced in their heads,

And Mama in her kerchief,
And I in my cap,
Had just settled down
For a long winter's nap,

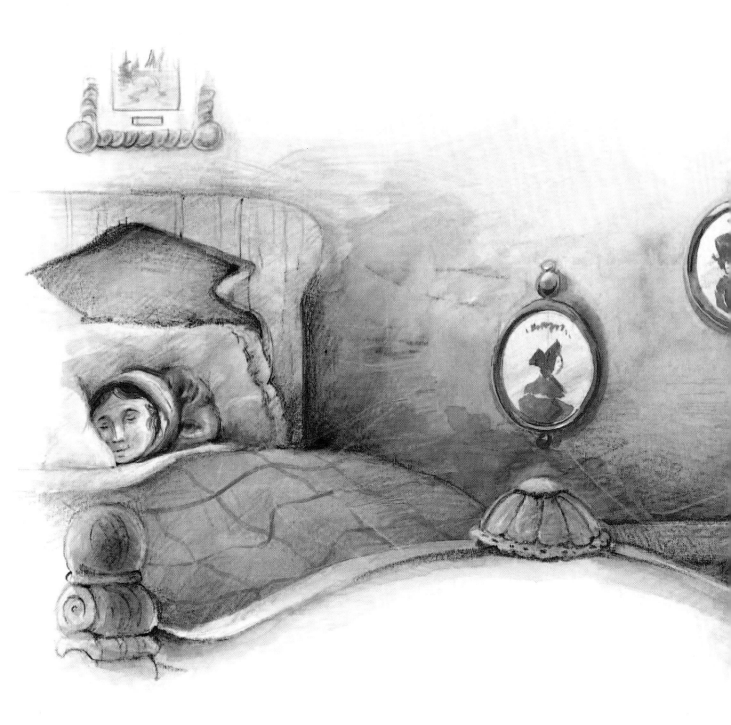

When out on the lawn
There arose such a clatter,
I sprang from my bed
To see what was the matter.

Away to the window
I flew like a flash,
Tore open the shutters
And threw up the sash.

The moon on the breast
Of the new-fallen snow
Gave a luster of midday
To objects below,

When, what to my wondering eyes
Should appear,
But a miniature sleigh
And eight tiny reindeer;

With a little old driver,
So lively and quick,
I knew in a moment
It must be St. Nick.

More rapid than eagles
His coursers they came.
And he whistled, and shouted,
and called them by name:

"Now, Dasher! now, Dancer!
Now, Prancer! and Vixen!
On, Comet! on, Cupid!
On, Donner and Blitzen!

To the top of the porch,
To the top of the wall!
Now dash away, dash away,
Dash away, all!"

As dry leaves that before
The wild hurricane fly,
When they met with an obstacle,
Mount to the sky,

So up to the house-top
The coursers they flew
With a sleigh full of toys,
And St. Nicholas, too.

And then in a twinkle,
I heard on the roof
The prancing and pawing
Of each little hoof.

As I drew in my head,
And was turning around,
Down the chimney St. Nicholas
Came with a bound.

He was dressed all in fur,
From his head to his foot,
And his clothes were all tarnished
With ashes and soot;

A bundle of toys
He had flung on his back,
And he looked like a peddler
Just opening his pack.

His eyes how they twinkled!
His dimples how merry!
His cheeks were like roses,
His nose like a cherry!

His droll little mouth
Was drawn up like a bow,
And the beard on his chin
Was as white as the snow.

The stump of a pipe
He held tight in his teeth,
And the smoke, it encircled
His head like a wreath.

He had a broad face
And a little round belly
That shook, when he laughed,
Like a bowl full of jelly.

He was chubby and plump,
A right jolly old elf.
And I laughed when I saw him,
In spite of myself.

A wink of his eye,
And a twist of his head,
Soon gave me to know
I had nothing to dread;

He spoke not a word,
But went straight to his work,
And filled all the stockings;
Then turned with a jerk,

And laying his finger
Aside of his nose,
And giving a nod,
Up the chimney he rose.

He sprang to his sleigh,
To his team gave a whistle,
And away they all flew
Like the down of a thistle.

But I heard him exclaim
As he drove out of sight,
"Happy Christmas to all
And to all a good night."